B.J.'s Billion-Dollar Bet

by Julie Anne Peters

Illustrated by Cynthia Fisher

SPRINGBOARD
B·O·O·K·S
®

Little, Brown and Company
Boston   New York   Toronto   London

To Mom
You raised us right

Text copyright © 1994 by Julie Anne Peters
Illustrations copyright © 1994 by Cynthia Fisher

First Edition

The characters and events portrayed in this book are fictitious.
Any similarity to real persons, living or dead, is coincidental and
not intended by the author.

Library of Congress Cataloging-in-Publication Data
Peters, Julie Anne.
    B.J.'s billion-dollar bet / by Julie Anne Peters.
        p.   cm. — (A Springboard book)
    Summary: When B.J. bets his mother's lottery ticket and
loses it to Mavis Mae, he will do anything to get it back
before Mavis Mae discovers it is the winning ticket.
    ISBN 0-316-70254-4 (hardcover, reinforced)
    [1. Lotteries — Fiction.   2. Wagers — Fiction.
3. Friendship — Fiction.]   I. Title.
PZ7.P44158Bj   1994
[Fic] — dc20   93-36132

Springboard Books and design is a registered trademark of
Little, Brown and Company (Inc.)

10 9 8 7 6 5 4 3 2 1

WOR

Published simultaneously in Canada
by Little, Brown & Company (Canada) Limited
PRINTED IN THE U.S.A.

1

B.J. Byner's eyes grew wide. "Could I try it?" He reached out a hand to Mavis Mae Clarry.

"Well . . ." She pursed her lips. "Okay, but don't run down the battery." She handed the blue plastic cylinder to B.J.

B.J. studied it up close. He'd never seen a real Grand Canyon six-color-ink pen with a dome-top flashlight before. Wow. It was cool. It had waves of water like the Colorado River and everything. B.J. flicked on the miniature flashlight. "Where'd you get it?"

"My grandma got it for me in Arizona," Mavis Mae said. "She just moved there, because of her asthma."

B.J. pushed down the purple button, and a ballpoint sprang out of the bottom. On his math paper he wrote his name in bright purple ink.

Mavis Mae asked, "Would it be okay with your dad if I had another Oreo?"

"Sure, go ahead." B.J. worked the first math problem, 28×11, in green ink.

"You got the wrong answer." Mavis Mae dropped a cookie crumb over his shoulder.

B.J. slapped a hand down on his paper. So what? he thought. It looks cool. What a great pen.

Mavis Mae sat across from B.J. at the kitchen table to finish her homework. The Clarrys had moved in down the street a couple of months ago. Since Mrs. Clarry was a single mom and had to work until five-thirty, B.J.'s dad had agreed to watch Mavis Mae after school.

"I think it's neat your dad stays home while your mom works." Mavis Mae cleared her place at the table.

B.J. shone the flashlight on Mavis Mae's silver barrettes. "Just don't call him Mr. Mom. He hates that."

She giggled. As she pulled her spelling notebook out of her backpack, she said, "Okay, give me back my pen."

B.J.'s fingers clasped it tightly. "Could I borrow it until tomorrow?"

"No way. You'll run down the battery."

"I promise I won't."

"Come on, B.J. Give it." She waggled her fingers at him.

B.J. clucked his tongue. Disgusted, he tossed the pen across the table to her. Selfish, he thought, as he watched her write *perpendicular* in her spelling notebook five times in pink ink.

B.J. had an idea. "You wanna trade?"

She peered up over her glasses. "Trade what?"

"Your pen."

"For what?"

"For . . ." He scanned the kitchen. "For the rest of the Oreos?"

She shook her head. "I'll get fat."

"Fat-*ter*," B.J. muttered under his breath. Then he had a brainstorm. "Hold on a second." He raced to his bedroom. A moment later he returned, lugging an enormous contraption in his arms. "How about trading for this?" He plunked it on the linoleum at her feet.

Mavis Mae dropped her jaw. Her glasses slid down her nose. "You're kidding. You want to trade my pen for your Batmobile?"

"Remote-controlled. Front and rear suspension, 9.6V turbo. Deal?"

Mavis Mae licked her lips. "Does it work?"

He sneered. "Of course it works. It just needs new batteries."

She looked from the pen to the Batmobile and back again. "Okay." She handed the pen to B.J.

He gave her the remote-control box. Just then B.J.'s dad staggered into the kitchen. An overflowing laundry basket was balanced in one arm while a two-ton box of Cheer stuck out from the other. "I just saw your mom drive up, Mavis Mae," he grunted. "Better gather up your stuff."

"Thanks, Mr. Byner." She dropped her spelling notebook into her backpack. "See you tomorrow, B.J. And thanks for the Batmobile." She bent down and hefted it up.

At the door B.J. flashed a quick SOS in flashlight code on the metal mailbox at the curb. As soon as Mavis Mae was out of earshot, he called out, "If that hunk of junk gets stuck in reverse again, just give it a good kick."

2

"Open up, John Elway." B.J. shone his flash-light down his guinea pig's throat. "Let me see your tonsils." John Elway squirmed on top of B.J.'s chest. He sniffed the pen, then started to nibble on the dome. Meanwhile, B.J. imagined himself racing a kayak down the Colorado River.

There was a knock on B.J.'s bedroom door. "I'm finishing my homework," he yelled.

The door burst open. Mavis Mae surged in, lugging the Batmobile. "I have to give this back." She plunked it down on B.J.'s hardwood floor. "My mom says I'm not allowed to trade." In a small voice she added, "Could I have my pen back?"

"Awww . . ." B.J. rolled the smooth cylinder between his fingers. Reluctantly, he handed it over.

"Sorry," Mavis Mae mumbled.

"Yeah." B.J. got up and set John Elway in his cage. He kicked the Batmobile into his closet.

"Can I pick John Elway up?" Mavis Mae asked.

"No." B.J. turned to meet her wounded eyes. "Oh, all right. But don't squeeze him."

She huffed. "B.J., I'm not a baby." She kiss-kissed at his guinea pig. B.J. winced. He gave a last swift kick to his Batmobile and heard it crash into the closet wall. Something, a bunch of things, flew out.

"Oh, I forgot about those," Mavis Mae said. "I put them in the Batmobile to save for later."

B.J.'s mouth began to water as he retrieved the three Tootsie Roll Pops from the floor. He loved Tootsie Roll Pops. But ever since his last dental checkup, when he'd come home with seven cavities, his parents wouldn't allow candy in the house.

He sniffed one of the suckers. Ah, cherry. Sneaking a peek toward the hall where his father was vacuuming, he whispered to Mavis Mae, "I'll trade you for these. You can have any one of those Micro Machines on my desk."

Mavis Mae glanced over B.J.'s cluttered desk. "I can't," she said. "If my mom found out . . ."

"Oh, yeah. Well, how about a bet? Your mom didn't say you couldn't bet, did she?"

Mavis Mae peered at him over her glasses. "What kind of bet?"

B.J. thought for a minute. "I bet if you set John Elway on the floor, he'll come running to me."

"Sure he will. He'll smell the Tootsie Roll Pops."

B.J. clucked. "Guinea pigs don't eat candy. But if you're worried about it, here. I'll stick them in my pocket." He jammed all the suckers into his back pocket.

"I don't know . . ." Mavis Mae hesitated.

"Look, if he doesn't come to me, you can pick another Micro Machine," B.J. said. The scent of grape wafted up his nose. "Make that two more."

Mavis Mae eyed the collection. "Okay. You're on."

She set John Elway down on the floor. Immediately, he began to nibble on a magazine.

"Come on, John Elway." B.J. slapped his knees. "Come on, boy." The guinea pig continued to chew. "Come on," B.J. called louder.

"He's not exactly tearing up the floor to get to you," Mavis Mae said. "In fact, the only

thing he's tearing up is your *Sports Illustrated For Kids*."

"What?" B.J. rushed across the room. He yanked his new November issue away, just as John Elway made Swiss cheese of Shaquille O'Neal's face.

Mavis Mae looked at her watch. "I better get going. I'll just take this one, this one, and" — she studied the row of Micro Machines — "this one."

Idiot, B.J. chided himself. Mavis Mae had such a big mouth. Tomorrow it'd be all over school how he'd been suckered by his own bet.

Mavis Mae paused in the doorway and smirked. "My Tootsie Roll Pops, pleeease?"

He yanked them out of his pocket. As B.J. smacked the last one into her outstretched palm, John Elway came skittering across the floor toward him, twitching his nose and screeching, "Vreet! Vreet!"

3

When B.J. climbed on the bus after school, he breathed a big sigh of relief. He hadn't been razzed once about losing the bet to Mavis Mae. Maybe she forgot, he thought. Too much sugar on the brain. B.J. snickered as he passed her sitting alone, as usual, her nose in a book.

Since it was Friday, B.J.'s dad let them watch *All-Star Wrestling* instead of doing homework. While B.J. tuned in the little portable TV in the kitchen, Mavis Mae chomped on their after-school snack. "Tomorrow's my birthday," she said, swallowing a bite of celery stick dipped in peanut butter. "I'm having a party."

"Yeah, so?" B.J. wiggled the antenna on top of the TV.

"So I thought you might like to come over later for cake and ice cream."

"With all those girls? Forget it."

Mavis Mae shrugged. "Suit yourself." She leaned forward on her elbows to watch the first match. After the wrestlers were introduced, she said, "Beast of Blubber's going to win."

"No way." B.J. sneered. "He can't beat Captain Crush. No one can."

"Wanna bet?"

B.J. couldn't believe it. Here was his chance to win his Micro Machines back. "Sure, I'll bet."

"I didn't mean a real bet," Mavis Mae began.

"Why not?" B.J. said. "Put your money where your mouth is."

She shot him a dirty look.

"What I mean is, put my Micro Machines

where your mouth is." That didn't sound right either. "At least give me a chance to win my cars back."

Mavis Mae crunched on her celery stick. "And what are *you* going to bet?"

From the TV Captain Crush slammed Beast of Blubber to the mat. He began to stomp on his beefy belly. B.J. said quickly, "I'll bet you my rat's jaw. It's genuine."

"Genuine plastic." She dipped her celery into the Skippy jar.

What would she want, he wondered, besides food? Then he noticed the bulletin board by the telephone. A sly smile crept across B.J.'s lips. "Would you bet for a billion dollars?" he asked.

Mavis Mae snorted. "Of course, conehead. But where do *you* plan to get a billion dollars?"

B.J. leaped to his feet. He yanked out a red pushpin from the corkboard and removed the ticket underneath. "Right here."

"What?" Mavis Mae scoffed. "A lottery ticket?"

"Not just a lottery ticket. It could be the winning lottery ticket."

"Oh, *right.*" She rolled her eyes.

"You never know. No one's won for three months. It's gotta be worth at least a billion dollars by now."

Mavis Mae licked off a swirl of Skippy. She wasn't biting.

Captain Crush jammed a knee into Beast of Blubber's back. When Beast screamed in agony and fell to the mat, B.J. knew the match was nearly over. "Afraid to bet, huh?" he taunted Mavis Mae. "Afraid to admit a fourth-grader might be smarter than a fifth-grader? Or that boys really do know more about sports than girls do?"

"B.J. Byner . . ." She narrowed her eyes at him. "All right, you're on."

From the TV came three sharp slaps on the mat. "Yes!" B.J. cheered, plunging his fist into the air.

Mavis Mae scootched back her chair and

stood up. "How worthless," she said. "I should have taken the rat's jaw." As she snatched the lottery ticket out of B.J.'s hand, she stuck out her tongue.

B.J. whipped his head around to the TV, just in time to see the referee raise Beast of Blubber's hand in the air. "The winner!" he declared.

Back in his bedroom, B.J. said to John Elway, "Can you believe it? Captain Crush getting a leg cramp at the very last second? Cripes."

All of a sudden there was a bloodcurdling scream from the kitchen. Clasping John Elway to his chest, B.J. raced down the hall.

B.J.'s big sister, Blake, was hanging up the phone. Their mother was sitting at the kitchen table, reading the newspaper, while their father stood over her with a pasta fork in his hand. Noodles bubbled on the stove.

B.J.'s mother's chest was heaving, and she

was pointing to the newspaper. "What's wrong, dear?" B.J.'s father said. He peered over her shoulder to read the headline. " 'Big Blizzard Expected Tonight.' Is that what you're worried about? Tomorrow's Saturday. You don't have to go to work."

She shook her head, gasping for air.

B.J.'s father frowned. "All right, dear. Take it easy. Stand up." He pulled her up. "Bend over. Breathe deeply."

Without warning, her head shot back, hair flying everywhere. "I won the lottery!" she shrieked. "We're rich! B.J." — she waggled a finger at him — "grab my lottery ticket. It's right behind you on the bulletin board."

B.J. gulped. In John Elway's ear he whispered, "Uh-oh."

4

B.J.'s mother screamed. "Where is it? I always pin it to the bulletin board. Every week. Same place."

"Mom, maybe you didn't buy a lottery ticket this week," Blake said. She was helping her mother remove all the notes and schedules and lists from the corkboard.

"Of course I did. I always buy one."

"How do you know you had the winning numbers?" B.J. asked. "I mean, without the ticket —"

"I always pick the same numbers." She rushed over to her purse and dumped it out on the table. "I pick our four birthdays, your father's and my anniversary, and my forever age, thirty-six."

B.J.'s father read the winning numbers from the newspaper. "Four, sixteen, twenty-two, twenty-five, thirty, and thirty-six."

They all checked the numbers in their heads. Then, sounding as if a bomb had hit the house, they exploded at once, "We're rich, rich, rich!" Hugging each other and jumping around the kitchen, they cheered and cheered.

B.J.'s mother wiped her eyes. "Now what did I do with that ticket?" she muttered.

B.J. dashed to his room. He slammed the door. What was he going to do? He couldn't trade for the ticket since Mavis Mae wasn't allowed. And she'd never give it back if she knew it was the winner. In his panic all he could think of was to try to win it back on another bet. He rummaged through his desk drawers until he found something Mavis Mae might want.

B.J. tore down the street to Mavis Mae's house on the corner. After a mumbled hello to her mother at the door, he flew up the stairs. Remembering the morning's headlines, he blurted out, "Bet you a silver steelie it's going to snow tonight." He held out his prized bag of marbles.

Mavis Mae continued to roll up a hunk of hair on a steamy curler. "What did you do?" she asked. "Look in the mirror and see a flake?" She giggled at her own joke.

B.J. clucked his tongue in disgust.

Mavis Mae spun around on her vanity seat. She squeezed the bag of marbles dangling from B.J.'s fist. Meanwhile, he searched her room for his mother's lottery ticket. He spotted it on the windowsill, where it was folded up in the shape of a frog.

Spinning back around, Mavis Mae said, "No, thanks. Who needs one steelie?"

B.J. rattled the bag. "Two then."

Mavis Mae didn't answer.

"Three." His voice rose to a squeak.

She wound her bangs around another curler.

"Okay. The whole bag."

She looked at him in the mirror. "What do you want from me?"

"How about those?" He pointed.

She followed his finger. "My origami animals?" Mavis Mae closed her curler kit, and sighed. "B.J., I don't really want to bet. It doesn't feel right."

B.J. eyed the windowsill again. "Then how much do you want for them?"

"The whole collection?"

"Uh, yeah," he stammered. He didn't want her to get suspicious. "I forgot I have an art project due on Monday."

Mavis Mae pursed her lips. She got up and went to the window. "The dragon folded out of a dollar bill isn't for sale." She whisked it away. "For the rest . . . twenty-five dollars."

"Twenty-five dollars! What a rip-off."

"It's art." Mavis Mae beamed. "You said so yourself."

B.J. scowled. "Ten," he said.

"Twenty," she countered. "And that's my final offer."

B.J. grumbled all the way down the stairs. Where was he going to get twenty dollars? And fast?

5

The next morning B.J. ambushed his sister coming out of the bathroom. "Can I borrow twenty bucks?"

She laughed.

"I can guarantee if you'll loan me twenty dollars today, I'll pay you back on Monday." By then they'd all be rich, and she probably wouldn't even remember the loan.

"Forget it," Blake said. "You still owe me fifteen bucks for the library book your stupid guinea pig mutilated."

"Don't call John Elway stupid. It's not my fault you left it on the floor by the TV. John Elway likes to snack while he watches *Wild America*."

A shadow passed behind them. "Dad, hey, Dad!" B.J. whirled to hail his father, who was hauling a basket of dry laundry down the hall. "Let me put those away for you," he offered. "I could clean the garage, too. And the basement. For an extra five bucks, I'll even pick up my room."

His dad paused and considered B.J. "When I asked you to sweep the garage last weekend you were too busy. Sorting baseball cards, wasn't it?"

"Come on, Dad."

"Sorry, B.J. I'm not going to pay you for doing chores."

B.J. clucked. "Well, how about my savings?"

His dad just looked at him.

"Yeah," B.J. groaned. "I know. College. But

who needs college if you're so rich you never have to work?"

"If that's your plan, you'd better go help your mother win the lottery."

"I'm trying," B.J. mumbled.

His dad disappeared into the bedroom. B.J. wandered out to the kitchen. His mother was sitting in the middle of the floor. Coupons and recipe cards were scattered everywhere.

"Mom?"

"Maybe I used it to mark my place in a cookbook," she said, blinking up at him. "I made that horrible salmon loaf two nights ago, remember?"

Did he ever. Barf-a-round.

"B.J., hand me that cookbook on the shelf, *Loads of Loafs,* will you?"

"Uh, Mom," he said, reaching for it.

She took the book from B.J., adding, "Might as well hand me all the others, too." She began to thumb through the cookbook pages, muttering to herself.

The doorbell rang, and B.J. went to answer it. It was Mavis Mae. "Can I borrow two eggs for my birthday cake?" she said. "Mom dropped a whole carton on the floor. What a mess."

"You should've asked my dad to make your cake," B.J. muttered, closing the door behind her. "He makes the best birthday cakes in the world."

"Your dad cooks, too?"

B.J. blushed. "Men can cook. Why not?"

Mavis Mae shrugged. "You're right. Hey, did you hear somebody won the lottery? It was on the news this morning."

B.J. gulped. "Uh, yeah. I heard. Sorry about that."

"Don't be sorry. No one's turned in the winning ticket yet. Maybe I won. Do you know the numbers?"

"No." The lie was out before B.J. could stop it.

"Well, could I look in your newspaper? Mom cleaned up the eggs with ours."

"Uh . . ." While he was trying to stall, Mavis Mae brushed by him. B.J. shot ahead of her. Good thing, too. The newspaper was open on the kitchen table with the lottery numbers circled in red.

"Wouldn't it be funny if I actually won with your lottery ticket?"

A real scream, B.J. thought. He scooped up the newspaper page and crumpled it in his fist.

Mavis Mae thumbed through the rest of the paper on the table. "I don't see them," she said. "Oh, well. I'll just have Mom catch the numbers on the news while I'm having my party. See you later, B.J."

Later that morning the news came on. "Turn it up, will you, B.J.?" his dad said.

B.J. twisted the volume knob. "And now for the local news. Apparently, we have a winner in the fifty-million-dollar lottery. But whoever it is chooses to remain anonymous. The winner should know that if the money isn't claimed by six P.M. Sunday, it will be forfeited."

B.J.'s mother muffled a scream. The announcer said, "Just to repeat, the winning lottery numbers are . . ."

B.J. scrambled for the phone.

"Hello?" Mavis Mae answered.

"Did you hear the lottery numbers on TV just now?" B.J. asked.

"No, I was busy." She sounded as if she'd been crying. "What are they?"

"Uh, I wasn't listening. I just thought maybe you heard."

Mavis Mae sniffled. B.J. hung up. What was her problem? he wondered. It couldn't be anything serious. Not like trying to get a winning lottery ticket back before the person who had it found out she was a billionaire.

6

B.J. found a Magic Marker in the junk drawer and headed for the garage to make a sign.

CAR WASH $5.00

He unfolded a lawn chair at the curb. "Four cars, that's all I need." Sprawling out, he locked his hands behind his head.

He waited. And waited. Eleven cars sped by. Not one stopped. "Maybe it's too cold," he said as he watched snow clouds gathering overhead. He had to do something.

A flake of snow melted on B.J.'s nose. After an hour, still no customers.

Another half hour crept by. B.J. uncorked his Magic Marker.

"How's business?" Mavis Mae loomed over the lawn chair.

"Why? What do you care?"

When she didn't answer, B.J. looked up at her. Her face was splotchy red. "Rough party?" he said.

She swallowed hard. "I came by to ask if you'd like to come over for cake."

"You mean there's some left? I told you my dad should've made it."

Mavis Mae bit her lip. "The whole cake's left. Nobody came to my party." She burst into tears and fled down the street.

B.J. felt bad. Really bad. He knew Mavis Mae wasn't the most popular girl in school. Not because she was a little overweight, either. Jason Gerard was a lot overweight, and everyone still liked him. No, Mavis Mae's problem was that she was such a know-it-all. A real show-off. "Just like Blake," B.J. thought out loud. Maybe that's why it didn't bother him so much; he was used to it. "Not one person came to her birthday party? Man." B.J. tossed his sign into the garbage can, re-coiled the hose, and walked over to the Clarrys' house.

Mavis Mae's mother answered the bell. "B.J." Her face brightened. "Come in. Mavis Mae and I were just about to celebrate her birthday." Mavis Mae appeared in the doorway, blowing her nose.

"I was washing cars down the street" — B.J. thumbed over his shoulder — "and I thought I smelled chocolate cake."

Mavis Mae giggled. As B.J. passed her on the way to the kitchen, she whispered, "Thanks. You're a good friend."

B.J. blushed.

They polished off most of the cake, plus a carton of rocky road ice cream. In the foyer Mavis Mae said, "My uncle got four tickets to the Nuggets game this afternoon. Do you want to go?"

B.J.'s eyes lit up. Not only did he want to go, it was the perfect opportunity. He was never going to earn twenty dollars by Sunday night. "Sure," he said. "On one condition."

Mavis Mae frowned. "What condition?"

"We make a bet on the game."

"B.J. —"

"Okay, forget it." He opened the door.

"Why do you keep doing this? You know I'll win."

He stepped onto the porch. A tug on his sweatshirt stopped him.

"If I don't bet, does that mean you won't want to be my friend anymore?"

B.J. felt a twinge of guilt. But he had no choice. Did he?

Mavis Mae sighed. "Okay. What do you want to bet?"

B.J. turned around slowly. "My marbles?"

"You've already lost those." She smirked.

B.J. rolled his eyes. At least she hadn't lost her sense of humor.

"I've got about a hundred cat's-eyes already, B.J.," she said. "Don't you have anything else?"

He thought hard. "What about my newest set of Topps baseball cards? There's a Bret Saberhagen."

"I think I got the same set," she answered.

B.J. was clean out of ideas. What would a girl want? What would his sister want if she were betting? He snapped his fingers. "How about a life-size poster of Arnold Schwarzenegger in a skimpy bikini?"

She arched an eyebrow. "Like the one on your sister's door?"

"Exactly."

Mavis Mae scootched her glasses up her nose. "Okay. What do you want?"

"Those paper thingies on your windowsill."

"My origami? I told you before, the dragon is out."

The dragon is peanuts, he said to himself. "Yeah, okay." He tried to look disappointed. "No dragon."

She sighed. "You've got a bet."

"I'll take the Nuggets," B.J. said. They were really hot right now. They'd just won ten games in a row.

Mavis Mae widened her eyes. "Do you know something I don't know?"

B.J. smiled. "Hard to believe, isn't it?"

7

B.J. stormed into the house. "Mavis Mae might have mentioned the Nuggets were playing the Chicago Bulls," he grumbled out loud. "Cripes. They got creamed."

B.J. heard his father call up from the basement, "Has the evening paper come yet?"

The paper? B.J. braced himself against the kitchen counter. Not the paper. He bolted for the door. Sure enough, newspapers were landing on porches up and down the block. B.J. charged down the sidewalk to Mavis Mae's, almost colliding with the newspaper delivery girl at the corner.

"Watch it," she said from her motor scooter. "And move, will ya? You're blocking my pitch." She reared back to sidearm the newspaper.

"Hold it." B.J. held out his hand. "I'll deliver that one. I'm going in there."

The girl snapped her gum at him and glared. "If I get a call from my boss saying the Clarrys never got their newspaper — kid, you're history." She plunked the paper in his hand.

"Ooh, I'm really scared." He sneered, though a tremor raced up his spine.

The scooter backfired and puttered away. B.J. unbanded the paper. He let it fan out over the frosted lawn. There it was, in the bottom right corner, a shaded box with the winning lottery numbers. He ripped off the corner. Most of the front page came with it. Rebanding the paper, he tossed it up onto the Clarrys' front porch.

A few minutes later Mavis Mae showed up on his doorstep. "Can you believe it? The front page of our paper was all torn up. My mom called the newspaper to complain."

"She didn't!" B.J. gulped.

"Could I see your paper? I just want to check the lottery numbers."

The paper was lying on the floor in front of the recliner, where B.J.'s father had been reading it. Mavis Mae flopped down on the carpet. "I'll just copy down the numbers." She pulled the Nuggets program from her pocket.

B.J. lunged for the paper. Accidentally, he knocked over his father's cup of coffee.

"B.J.!" Mavis Mae yelped. She jumped to her feet, brushing off her jeans. "You're such a klutz."

"Sorry." B.J. shrugged. But as he watched the lottery numbers smear together in a pool of coffee, it was hard to hide his grin.

*   *   *

On Sunday morning Blake came stomping into the kitchen. "Somebody stole my Arnold Schwarzenegger poster!" she yowled.

B.J. slid down his chair, trying to look invisible.

Blake grabbed a fistful of B.J.'s hair.

"Hey, I don't have your stupid poster," he said. It was the truth, sort of. He'd sneaked it out after she'd left on a date last night. Just as Blake was about to make mashed potatoes of B.J.'s head, a pitiful whimper sounded from the doorway. B.J. and Blake turned to look. Their father was helping their mother into the kitchen.

"Sit here, dear," he said. "I'll brew you a cup of tea. Nice hot tea to calm your nerves."

"Tea?" She whipped up her head, tangled hair flying every which way. "I haven't looked through the tea bags. Or the cereal boxes or the cupboards . . ." She flew across the kitchen.

"No ticket yet, huh?" Blake whispered to her father.

He shook his head sadly. "Your mother's a basket case. Just look at her."

B.J. thought she looked like a zombie from *Night of the Living Dead*. He swallowed hard as he watched her rip open all the tea bags, one by one.

Back in his bedroom, B.J. told John Elway, "Mom's a goner if I don't do something quick."

John Elway screeched, "Vreet!" B.J. hugged him to his chest. "You're worried too, aren't you? I've got to tell Mom the truth about the ticket. She's going to kill me. So is Dad. And after Blake finds out I gave her Arnold poster to Mavis Mae, she'll get her licks in, too. Man. I'm dead."

B.J. shot up to a sitting position. "Unless . . ."

8

Mavis Mae was still dressed up from church as she trailed B.J. down the hall. From the kitchen a TV announcer's voice said, "Let me repeat. The winning lottery numbers are four, sixteen . . ."

Mavis Mae paused behind B.J. "Listen," she said.

"Come on," B.J. urged. "I said I had something to show you."

"Shhh." She cupped a hand around her ear.

"Twenty-two, twenty-five," she repeated after the announcer.

B.J. rattled off, "Eighteen, ninety-nine, hundred and six, forty-three . . ."

"Quit it." Mavis Mae whapped his arm. "Oh, shoot. Now I lost the numbers."

B.J. exhaled a loud sigh of relief.

Mavis Mae narrowed her eyes at him. "Why do I get the sneaking suspicion you don't want me to know those lottery numbers?"

B.J. gulped. "That's crazy. I'll tell you the numbers. They're four, sixteen, twenty-two, twenty-five, thirty . . . and uh, forty."

While casting him a dubious look, Mavis Mae wrote down the numbers. Hastily, B.J. ushered her into his room. He checked the hall. The coast was clear. The only sound was a muffled sobbing coming out of his parents' bedroom. B.J. shut the door.

"So, did you finish your art project?" Mavis Mae asked.

"My what? Oh, that. No. I'll just flunk art. So what?" He kicked a shoe into the closet while peering over his shoulder at Mavis Mae. She didn't look very sorry, like he'd hoped. "I'm no good in art," he added. "Not like you."

She beamed.

B.J. brushed by her and knelt on the floor beside the bed. From underneath he pulled out a square wooden box. When he opened it, Mavis Mae gasped.

"It's my dad's," B.J. said. "He won it in a chess tournament in college." B.J. crossed his fingers behind his back. "He's giving it to me for my birthday next month." Don't I wish, B.J. thought.

Mavis Mae picked up the queen piece, carved out of white marble. "Gorgeous," she breathed.

"Do you know how to play?"

She tossed her head. "Of course."

He knew she'd say that. B.J. began to set up the chessboard. "How about a game?"

Mavis Mae peered at him over her glasses. "For a bet, right?"

He shook his head. "No way. Just a friendly game. I'm not a very good player. Probably not as good as you."

"At least you admit it. No betting? Honest?"

"Nope. Scout's honor." He held up two fingers. Okay, so he'd never been a scout. She didn't know that.

He let Mavis Mae win the first game, easy. The second game he let her capture most of his pieces. That took about ten minutes. Then she won the next game, and the next.

Mavis Mae yawned. "I'd better be getting home."

"Wait!" B.J. cried. "One more game. For a, uh, small wager?"

She looked at him. He shrugged. "Hey, I'm desperate."

Mavis Mae shook her head. "No kidding. Do your parents know you're a compulsive gambler?"

He didn't reply. "I guess you know what I want. And you can have anything in this room," he told her.

Mavis Mae arched an eyebrow. "Including the chess set?"

B.J. smiled weakly. "I said anything." He felt guilty about tricking Mavis Mae. But then the image of his poor mother flashed through his head. "Set up the board," he said.

Fifteen minutes into the game, B.J. started to sweat. The match was close. Closer than he'd expected. He had to call on all his best moves to outplay Mavis Mae. Finally, he saw his chance and took it. "Check." He grinned.

Mavis Mae didn't hesitate. She captured his knight with her queen. "Checkmate," she declared.

B.J. studied the board. He clucked his tongue. He clucked again. "Cheater."

Mavis Mae leaped to her feet. She put her hands on her hips. "B.J. Byner. You know I didn't cheat!"

B.J. mumbled, "I know. Sorry." To himself he added, Am I ever going to be sorry. He shoved the chess set toward her. "Go ahead. Take it."

Mavis Mae shook her head. "Never mind the chess set. I want that." She pointed.

"No way!" B.J. cried.

"You said anything in this room. And that's what I want."

At the door, B.J. choked back his tears. "Good-bye," he called down the sidewalk. "Good-bye, John Elway."

9

B.J. faced his family across the dinner table. His mother was staring off into space, whimpering with each intake of breath. His father was studying her, looking worried. His sister was swirling gravy through the mashed potatoes in her microwave dinner.

The reporter on the five-thirty news was reminding everyone that the lottery winner had only one half hour to go. B.J.'s mother began to cry. "It's all my fault," she wailed. Blake patted her shoulder. "It's okay, Mom. Don't blame yourself." B.J.'s heart pounded as he set down his fork. "Mom, Dad, Blake, I have a confession to make."

All eyes locked on him. "You may have noticed a few things missing around here —"

The doorbell rang. Saved by the bell, B.J. thought, jumping to his feet.

His father caught him by the arm. "Blake, will you please answer the door? Now, you were saying, B.J.? About things missing?"

B.J. tugged on the T-shirt that seemed to be tightening around his neck. Just as he was about to speak, Blake reappeared in the doorway. And she wasn't alone.

Standing behind her were Mavis Mae and her mother. Mavis Mae looked mad. "Go ahead," her mother said, handing her a cardboard box.

Mavis Mae thrust it at B.J. "Here. Mom says I can't keep any of this stuff I won from you on bets. I wasn't going to keep John Elway. I was just trying to teach you a lesson."

"Hey, that looks like my Arnold Schwarzenegger poster." Blake pulled the rolled-up poster out of the box. "It *is* my poster."

"B.J.," his father roared, rising from his seat. "What is going on here?"

"It was just a little bet," B.J. squeaked.

"It wasn't all B.J.'s fault," Mavis Mae said. "I was partly responsible."

"Yes, she was," Mrs. Clarry agreed. "That's why she's being punished."

B.J. watched as tears filled Mavis Mae's eyes. He'd never felt so crummy in his life. None of this was Mavis Mae's fault. Boy, what a friend *he* was.

"Go put that stuff in your room," B.J.'s dad ordered. "Then get back in here. I want a full explanation."

Before B.J. left, he motioned Mavis Mae aside. "I'm really sorry," he said. "I didn't mean to get you in trouble."

Mavis Mae just glowered.

B.J. added, "I really do like your origami ani-

mals. Especially the dragon. Maybe you can teach me how to make one."

She eyed him coolly. "Yeah, sure. Some year when I'm not grounded."

"Let's go, Mavis Mae," her mother called.

Mavis Mae turned and followed her mother through the living room. Watching her close the front door, B.J. thought, As soon as I hand over the winning lottery ticket, everyone is going to forget about all this and I'll be a hero. Mavis Mae will want to be my friend again. Everything will get back to normal.

He heard his mother rip open a new box of Kleenex. Then he saw the fire in his sister's eyes and the set jaw on his father's face. And he wasn't so sure.

10

B.J. lifted John Elway out of the box. He kissed the top of his fuzzy head. John Elway didn't even coo. In fact, he looked kind of mad.

"B.J.!" his dad hollered from the kitchen. "Get in here."

"Don't move." B.J. set his guinea pig back down. "We need to talk." He raced out the door. Halfway to the kitchen he remembered the lottery ticket.

"B.J.!"

He didn't dare go back.

"Sit down, young man," his father said.

"But, Dad —"

"*No* buts. We have a very serious matter to discuss here," his father began. "Gambling."

B.J. glanced up at the kitchen clock. It was five to six. "Dad —"

His father held up a hand. "I don't want to hear any excuses. Gambling in the first place is bad enough, but gambling with other people's property —"

"Yeah, like my Arnold poster." Blake glared at him.

"Not to mention your own guinea pig."

B.J. hung his head.

"Gambling is a disease," his father went on. "You know your poor uncle Arlo? He used to be your rich uncle Arlo until he lost his entire life savings in Las Vegas . . ."

Visions of Corvettes and speedboats and swimming pools swam through B.J.'s brain. Finally, he couldn't stand it anymore. "I've got Mom's lottery ticket," he blurted out.

"*What?*" His father's eyes popped wide open. Then, as the news sank in, he asked, "Where is it?"

"In my room."

Everyone gasped. "Well, go get it." B.J.'s father shot up. "I'll call the lottery office."

B.J. dashed back to his bedroom. He reached in the box for the origami frog. It wasn't there. He clawed through the Micro Machines and marbles. Suddenly, a flash of white caught his eye and he screamed, "John Elway, no!"

He yanked the paper frog out of John Elway's mouth. Most of the head was chewed off. When B.J. unfolded the ticket, his whole body sagged.

Back in the kitchen, B.J. tugged on his father's sleeve. "Hang up, Dad." B.J. showed him the ticket. Four of the numbers had been completely chewed away.

Blake snatched the ticket out of his hand. "B.J.!" she blasted him. She showed the ticket to their mother, who stared at it in shock.

"It's all my fault," B.J. said. He explained how he'd lost the ticket on a bet with Mavis Mae and tried to get it back. All the rotten tricks he'd pulled. "I'm really sorry," B.J. finished, his voice faltering.

B.J.'s mother gave him a hug.

"B.J., I'm tempted to punish you," B.J.'s father said, "but I think you realize how serious this is. And maybe the way you feel, the way you're going to feel for a long time, is punishment enough."

B.J. nodded, fighting back his tears.

Looking around the table at all the gloomy faces, Mr. Byner added, "Hey, come on. I think we've learned a valuable lesson here."

"Yeah. Never have a brother," Blake muttered.

"No. Gambling makes you crazy."

B.J. met his father's eyes.

"You did the right thing, son, by telling us the truth." He opened his arms to include everyone. "And, as far as I'm concerned, we already are a million-dollar family."

B.J. held John Elway up to his face. "Can you ever forgive me?" he asked.

John Elway nuzzled up under B.J.'s chin. "Thanks, buddy. Now I wonder if Mavis Mae will ever forgive me. Or Mom. Or Blake." Even though they weren't rich, and he had lots of making up to do, B.J. felt relieved it was over. "From now on," he declared, "I'm out of the betting business."

He set John Elway in his cage. Then B.J. picked up the half-eaten lottery ticket. "Well, maybe just one more bet."

B.J. dropped the ticket into John Elway's food dish. "John Elway," he said. "I bet you're going to be the only billion-dollar guinea pig in the world."

John Elway scampered toward the dish, screeching, "Vreet, vreet!"